MOO MOO

Moo Moo & Mr. Quackers present

What's Cooking, Moo Moo?

A Tim Miller Production

Brought to you by

BALZER + BRAY
An Imprint of HarperCollinsPublishers

Balzer + Bray is an imprint of HarperCollins Publishers.

Moo Moo & Mr. Quackers Present: What's Cooking, Moo Moo?
Copyright © 2018 by Tim Miller
All rights reserved. Manufactured in China.

Library of Congress Control Number: 2017934753
ISBN 978-0-06-241441-0

Typography by Dana Fritts
The pictures in this book were made with brush and ink and digital hocus-pocus.
18 19 20 21 22 SCP 10 9 8 7 6 5 4 3 2 1
❖
First Edition

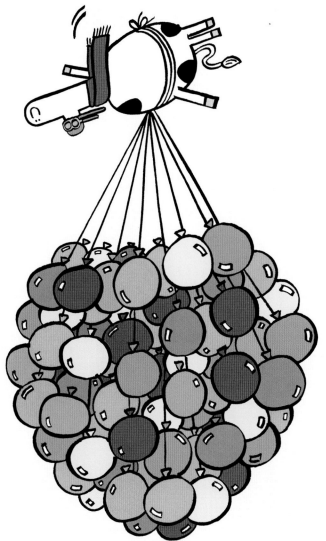

For Nancy (again)

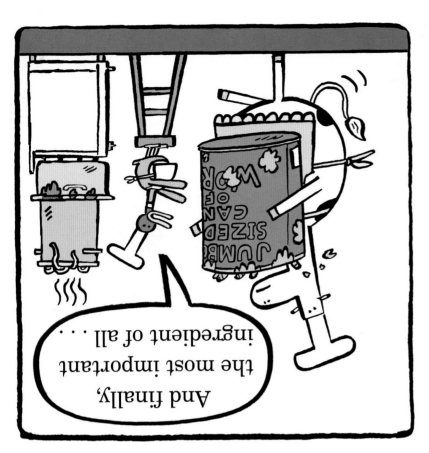

MR. QUACKERS